W9-AMS-052

A Beginning-to-Read Book

Up, Up, and Away

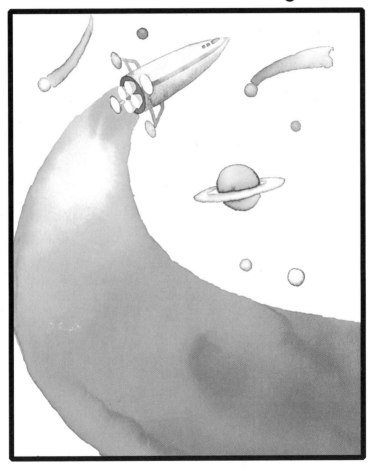

by Margaret Hillert

Illustrated by Robert Masheris

DEAR CAREGIVER, The *Beginning-to-Read* series is a carefully written collection of classic readers you may remember from your own childhood. Each book features text comprised of common sight words to provide your child ample practice reading the words that appear most frequently in written text. The many additional details in the pictures enhance the story and offer the opportunity for you to help your child expand oral language and develop comprehension.

Begin by reading the story to your child, followed by letting him or her read familiar words and soon your child will be able to read the story independently. At each step of the way, be sure to praise your reader's efforts to build his or her confidence as an independent reader. Discuss the pictures and encourage your child to make connections between the story and his or her own life. At the end of the story, you will find reading activities and a word list that will help your child practice and strengthen beginning reading skills.

Above all, the most important part of the reading experience is to have fun and enjoy it!

Shannon Cannon

Shannon Cannon,
Literacy Consultant

Norwood House Press • P.O. Box 316598 • Chicago, Illinois 60631
For more information about Norwood House Press please visit our website at
www.norwoodhousepress.com or call 866-565-2900.

LIBRARY OF CONGRESS CATALOGING-IN-PUBLICATION DATA
Hillert, Margaret.
  Up, up, and away / Margaret Hillert ; illustrated by Robert Masheris. —
Rev. and expanded library ed.
    p. cm. — (Beginning-to-read series)
  Summary: "Two children travel to the moon in a spaceship, do some
exploring, and come back home again"—Provided by publisher.
  ISBN-13: 978-1-59953-151-9 (library edition : alk. paper)
  ISBN-10: 1-59953-151-8 (library edition : alk. paper) [1. Space flight to
the moon—Fiction. 2. Moon—Exploration—Fiction.] I. Masheris, Robert,
ill. II. Title.
  PZ7.H558Up 2008
  [E]—dc22   2007034739

Beginning-to-Read series (c) 2009 by Margaret Hillert.
Library edition published by permission of Pearson Education, Inc. in
arrangement with Norwood House Press, Inc. All rights reserved.
This book was originally published by Follett Publishing Company in 1982.

Look at this.
Here is something big.
What is it?
What can it do?

It can go up.
It can go up, up, up.
It can go up, up, and away.
And we can go up in it!

What fun!
What fun!
We will go up in it.
We will go away, away.

Come here.
Come here.
Here is a little car.
It will take us up to
where we want to go.

Here we are.
Get out. Get out
and go in here.
Here is where we go.

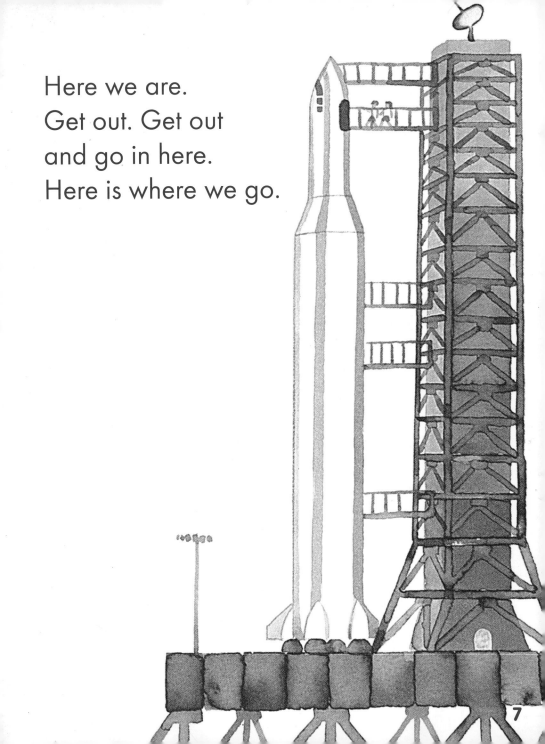

Now do this.
We have to do this.
It is good to do.
It will help us.

And away we go!

Here we go.
Up, up, and away to see
what we can see.

Oh, oh, oh!
What a ride this is!
What a good, good ride!

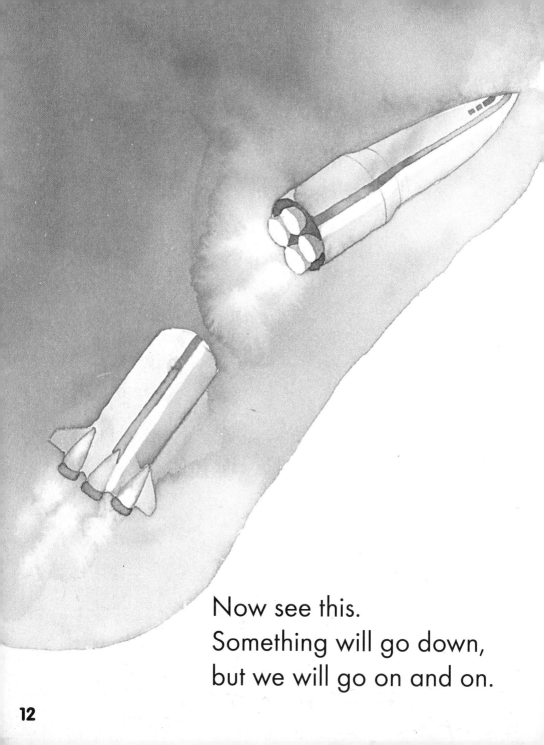

Now see this.
Something will go down,
but we will go on and on.

This one will go down, too.
But we are up here,
and we will go and go.

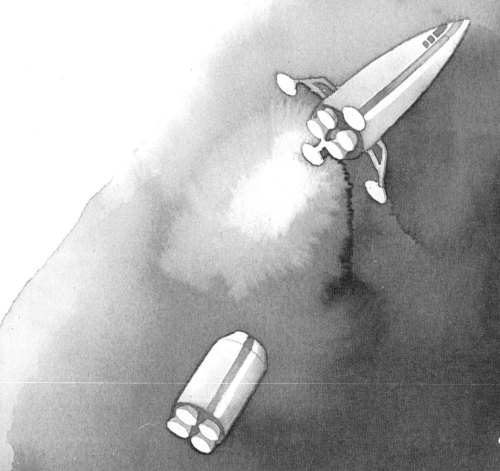

Look out here.
Look, look.
Look what I see.
Do you see that?

And now look here.
That is where we want to go.
We want to see what it
looks like.

Here we are.
Oh, here we are.
We will go down, down.
We will get out.
We will find out what
is here.

Oh, what big jumps!
What big jumps we can
take up here!
This is fun.

Get into this little car.
Now we will take a ride
to see what we can see.

Look here. Look here.
Down, down we go.
Way down in here.

And now look.
Up, up we go.
Way up here.

Look what we can see.

I guess I want to go now.
I want to see my house.
I want to see my mother
and father.
Do you want to go, too?

Get in. Get in.
We will go away now.

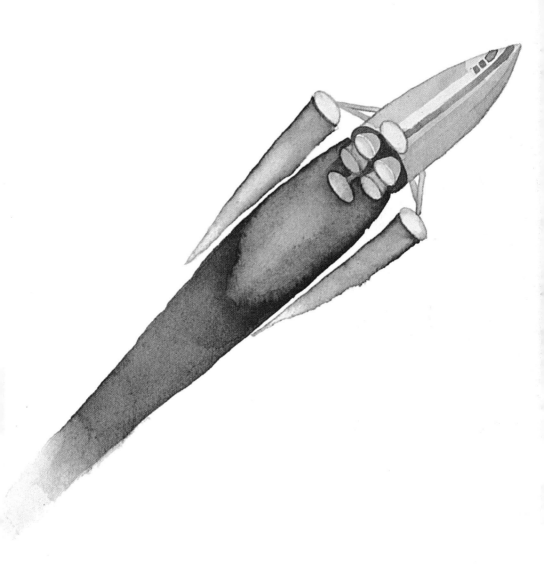

Down we go.
Down, down, down.
Here we come to a good spot.
This is a good spot for us.

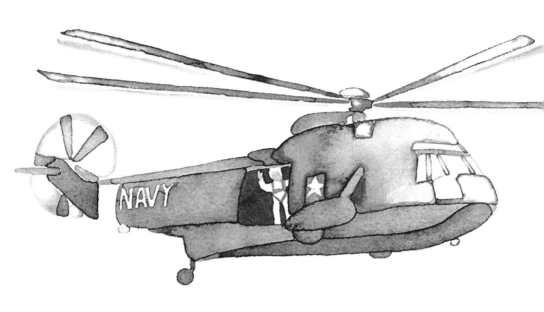

We are down now.
See the boat.
Here comes a boat.
It will get us.
That is good.

The following activities support the findings of the National Reading Panel that determined the most effective components for reading instruction are: Phonemic Awareness, Phonics, Vocabulary, Fluency, and Text Comprehension.

Phonemic Awareness: The /ōō/ sound

Sound Substitution: Say the words on the left to your child. Ask your child to repeat the word, changing the middle sound to the /ōō/ (as in moon) sound:

man=moon	hop=hoop	tot= toot	blah=blue
tray=true	dim=doom	tab=tube	grow=grew
blow=blew	cop=coop	fall=fool	rim=room
snip=snoop	flat=flute	now=new	

Phonics: Word Ladder

1. Word ladders are a fun way to build words by changing just one letter at a time.

2. Write the word **at** on a piece of paper and give your child the following step-by-step instructions (letters in between the // marks indicate that you are to give the sound as a clue rather than providing the actual letter):

   • Add the /s/ sound to the beginning of the word. What do you have? (sat)

   • Change the /s/ to a /p/. What do you have? (pat)

   • Change the /t/ to an /n/. What do you have? (pan)

   • Add an /l/ after the /p/. What do you have? (plan)

   • Add an e at the end. What do you have? (plane)

   • Add a /t/ at the end. Now what word do you have? (planet)

Vocabulary: Adverbs

1. Explain to your child that some words help us to understand where (or when) something happens. These words are called adverbs. They "add" to the verb by telling us where the verb happens.

2. Write the following words on separate pieces of paper:

up   away   above   here
down   far   near   now

3. Read each word to your child.

4. Mix up the words.

5. Read each of the following sentences. Say the underlined adverb in the sentence and ask your child to point to the piece of paper that has the adverb. Ask your child to name the verb that the adverb is describing.

- The girl and boy wanted to go up. (go)
- Here we are. (are)
- They will go away. (go)
- They looked above to see the moon. (looked)
- Something went down. (went)
- They flew far in the shuttle. (flew)
- They came near the stars. (came)
- It was time to go now. (go)

Fluency: Shared Reading

1. Reread the story to your child at least two more times while your child tracks the print by running a finger under the words as they are read. Ask your child to read the words he or she knows with you.

2. Reread the story taking turns, alternating readers between sentences or pages.

Text Comprehension: Discussion Time

1. Ask your child to retell the sequence of events in the story.

2. To check comprehension, ask your child the following questions:

- Is this story real? How do you know?
- Where did the girl and boy go?
- What did they see and do?
- Would you like to be an astronaut? Why or why not?

WORD LIST

Up, Up, and Away uses the 60 words listed below.

This list can be used to practice reading the words that appear in the text. You may wish to write the words on index cards and use them to help your child build automatic word recognition. Regular practice with these words will enhance your child's fluency in reading connected text.

a	fun	like	take
and		little	that
are	get	look(s)	the
at	go		this
away	good	mother	to
	guess	my	too
big			
boat	have	now	up
but	help		us
	here	oh	
can	house	on	want
car		one	way
come(s)	I	out	we
	in		what
do	into	ride	where
down	is		will
	it	see	
father		something	you
find	jumps	spot	
for			

ABOUT THE AUTHOR Margaret Hillert has written over 80 books for children who are just learning to read. Her books have been translated into many different languages and over a million children throughout the world have read her books. She first started writing poetry as a child and has continued to write for children and adults throughout her life. A first grade teacher for 34 years, Margaret is now retired from teaching and lives in Michigan where she likes to write, take walks in the morning, and care for her three cats.

Photograph by Glenna Washburn

ABOUT THE ADVISER Shannon Cannon contributed the activities pages that appear in this book. Shannon serves as a literacy consultant and provides staff development to help improve reading instruction. She is a frequent presenter at educational conferences and workshops. Prior to this she worked as an elementary school teacher and as president of a curriculum publishing company.